I0619653

DARKNESS DESCENDS

Book I

The Divide

Marta Moran Bishop

ISBN: 978-1939484376

Cover by Jade Lazlow

This book is dedicated to all the men and women, past and present, who have and will fight to promote equality and honor in our country, and to those who continue to fight for our freedom.

I want to thank my husband Ken for his continued support of my writing, often taking on more than his share of the household chores and losing me for hours at a time, as I sit at my computer.

A special thank you to my editor, Franki deMerle, and Jade Lazlo who are and continue to be an inspiration to me.

Chapter One

Slamming the door behind him, Dwight snarled at Sanders. "I bet that Bitch believed her famous football hero of a husband would save her."

"I'm sure she was in shock when he didn't even show up at the first trial. Sanders said with a smirk. Guess he couldn't be bothered, after all, she's just a woman."

With a loud burst of raunchy laughter, Dwight said. "He renounced her. Completely and totally for the bitch, she is. I was there on guard and heard the entire thing, and then he just turned and walked out before the guards brought her in."

The barest trace of light entered through the tiny, barred window, into the little cell. It was just enough light to make out Rebecca's form, lying in a heap on the dirt floor of the small cement room. Her appearance was horrible—almost unrecognizable. Still, she lifted her head slightly at the sound of the guard's conversation. "Darling Ben, I know that

1

must have been the hardest thing you've ever done, but thank you for keeping your promise to me, Jewell will now be safe." She whispered through cracked lips.

Gone was her long, shiny, straight, black hair, smooth brown skin, startling green eyes, and aquiline nose. Her hair, now a matted mass of blood, sweat, and tangled plaits, no longer did it hang in neat braids, flowing down her back. Instead, an unrecognizable mass of black, tangled and knotted filth partially covered her bruised, swollen and bloody face. Rebecca's aquiline nose broken, and only a few chipped teeth left in her mouth. Her startling green eyes were barely identifiable through the black and blue lumps of flesh, puffy from the multiple blows to her face, as the guards played their games, tossing her to one another.

Fighting to keep her sanity, Rebecca drifted in and out of consciousness. At times, she no longer felt her body. Instead, she floated somewhere above and into the magic of the universe. With each blow, her mind returned further and further into the past.

Chapter Two

"You must listen, Rebecca. These ceremonies are important. They aren't just the old traditions of our people; they are full of magic that can change the world. It is vital you feel the power of the between times."

"Father, I know. You've told me the same thing a million times, but I can't do it. I have tried and tried to no avail," the young girl said sadly.

Kinard's strong, bronzed hands reached for her, and he placed his long fingers on her slender shoulders. "Becca, I know you have spent all summer taking classes so that you can go to college in the fall, and every evening you spend with your mother learning the art of weaving according to her traditions, but you must also acquire the power of both the Celtic and my Native American cultures. Someday you will need to pass these things on to your daughter.

Yes, I said daughter, because that is what you will have. She will be a jewel amongst women," softly, he said as he looked into her face. Her aquiline nose, straight black hair, the promise of height, and the long dark lashes that framed her green eyes clearly showed her Native American heritage. The dusting of freckles across her nose and over her cheekbones along with those crystal-clear green eyes came from her Celtic background. She had Ana's eyes and freckles, but except for the slenderness of Becca's bone structure, it was apparent she was Native American.

Kinard stood and lifted Rebecca to her feet. "Come dance with me." His leather moccasins barely touched the ground as he raised one hand to the sky, palm upward, almost beckoning the universe to join them. His other hand held hers. His chiseled features and piercing black eyes lifted upward to absorb the softness of the dew-filled air. A low chant rumbled from deep within him and beckoned her feet to move with his. Slowly, her slender arm lifted, almost of its own accord, and her feet moved in time with his. The power of the air and earth filled them. Gone, were the enormous trees that surrounded them. The moon still clung to the night sky, radiant as it fought the sun for dominance. It was neither night, nor day, but somehow both, when the power of the between times descended into the dancers.

As dawn broke, the two of them stood with arms still out, bodies swaying, their faces glowing with an inner fire. Neither wanted to break the sacred silence and end the glow and joy of the connection that came from the time between worlds. They stood still, hand in hand, for a moment. The sound of the morning dove began, and the last hoot of the owl died off before they turned and walked back through the trees. Their feet barely touched the ground as they climbed up the hill to the small log cabin that nestled between the towering pines.

"Breakfast is calling," Kinard said softly, breaking the spell of the moment.

Chapter Three

"How did it go?" Ana asked inquisitively.

"Oh momma, I felt it today! The magic of the between times. I don't know if I will ever be able to control it though," she said wistfully.

"Maybe someday, dear heart," Ana answered, her red hair shimmering in the luminescent light, filling the room. "How swiftly the sun rises here at the lake, Kinard," she said looking at her husband's chiseled features. His high cheekbones and full lips became more apparent as he pulled his long black hair away from his face and braided it with the ease of long practice.

Rebecca brought an air of excitement that was palatable to the oak table, as the three sat down to eat.

Ana thought as she gazed at the two of them, *Kinard says it will be her daughter who will weave the magic into cloth and control the between times, though it cannot happen if Rebecca doesn't know how to pull in the power. You can see her resemblance to me only in the sprinkling of freckles across her face, her green eyes, and the slenderness of her frame, though she will have her father's height.*

For a few minutes, only the sound of silverware scraping plates and the crackle of the fire could be heard in the quiet of the morning.

Kinard thought to himself, *Rebecca will turn fifteen tomorrow. It's good that she was able to touch the power today.*

"Becca, tomorrow your father thought we could take the horses out and have a picnic in the glen for your birthday," Ana said as she looked at her husband. "You have been working hard all summer with the extra classes you are taking to get ready for college as well as learning to weave and work with both the old magic of the Celts and the Native Clans of your father's people. "We are very proud of you," Ana said.

Kinard looked at his wife and daughter. Love filled his soul, and in a deep voice, he stated calmly, "Although by the standards of American society you are very young, in our clans you are now a woman. In another week, you will go away to college."

Blushing, Rebecca smiled and raised her head high. "I know my life is about to change, but I want you both to know I love you and I'll never forget."

"Life will soon bring a husband your way," Ana said softly. I have seen it. I will not describe him to you, for you should not recognize him from a description but know him in your heart and soul. Suffice it to say he will bring with him a different form of magic, one that dates back thousands of years. And although he won't understand it, you must teach him how to reach it deep inside himself. It won't matter if he doesn't know how to use it, because the magic of his and your heritages will create one who can." Ana's voice held the sound of a prophecy.

"Momma, I'm too young to think of marriage."

"Yes dear, but it will happen. Oh, not for a while yet, maybe not for a year or two. You will be much too busy with your books and studies for a time. Each thing happens in its proper time. Now off with you, dear. Your father and I have things to do, and you could use some time with your friends down at the lake."

Chapter Four

A chilly rain fell, twelve-year-old Jamie had gotten tickets to watch the Bears play the Packers at Soldiers Field, and it appeared he sometimes hung out with Ben, the best tight end in football. At seventeen, Rebecca's friends thought her stupid for hanging out with him. But she felt comfortable with Jamie, and he was brilliant. He had to be. After all, at twelve-years-old, he was already in college and far ahead of her in his studies, to boot.

She knew he had a crush on her, but Becca knew he wasn't the one. And then she saw Ben, even though he was on the sidelines talking to the coach. For one brief moment, he looked up, and their eyes met. It was magic, and in that split second, Rebecca knew he felt it too. The crowds were noisily ushering out of the stadium, when Jamie said: "Come on Becca, in a few minutes we can go down to the locker room.

"Jamie, the men will be showering and dressing. It would be unseemly for me to go in, even though female reporters do, I am only seventeen, and I don't believe they'd feel comfortable about me in there."

"Ah, I guess you are right Becca, how about we meet up with Ben and some of the others at their hangout a bit later. I know it's usually only for older people, but my dad owns part of the Bears, and I can get us in. We might want to wait a bit though, at least until the crowds die down."

"Do you think it will be okay, Jamie? After all, wouldn't we be kind of breaking in on their celebration?"

"It'll be okay Becca. I saw how you and Ben looked at each other and as much as I wish it were me, you looked at that way. I know it never will be, so I might as well play cupid." He said, laughing.

After that night, the three of them were inseparable, but soon Jamie began to spend more time with his books, leaving them time to get to know each other. They rode, swam in the lake, teased each other mercilessly, ate, and talked for hours. Each day, Ben went to practice, and she spent hours at her studies or in class. It seemed as if they could never get enough time together. "Ben, it's beyond me how you managed to duck the paparazzi today. I hate the constant flashes of the cameras in my face all the time, and the whispers of my classmates do get to me."

"Darling, do you think we shouldn't see each other quite so much? We could pretend we broke up for a bit, and wait till things settle down again?"

"Don't ever say something like that again. I know I'd be completely miserable if I couldn't see you, even if it was temporary. Besides, do you truly think it would help? The tabloids would only print worse garbage about us. The speculation about what happened would go on and on, and there would be so many questions asked constantly."

"You're right. It wouldn't stop them or the whispers either. I think a part of it is the age difference between us. It's a good thing your parents gave their blessing, or someone would have me in court, even though we haven't yet...."

Both of their faces were covered in a deep red blush. They'd been dating now for a year and lordy, how hard it was to keep their hands off each other. But soon it would be Becca's eighteenth birthday, and she would no longer be jailbait. But my God, the rumors did spread, why even his coach had questioned him extensively about their relationship.

Ben's face got solemn just remembering that conversation. *"No sir, it's completely platonic.*

"Are you aware of how it looks?"

"Yes sir, but we are waiting. She is too young, and though I believe she loves me as I do her, Rebecca will have the chance to make sure, and there is her age."

"Be careful son; there are those who would like to see you harmed. Frankly, there is always someone who'd prefer someone else be hurt so that they can feel some deep-seed sense of vindication. It's a miserable thing."

"I will be vigilant coach. We always have someone else around, even when we'd rather be alone. We stick to public

places and events and make sure we are seen going our separate ways. I wouldn't want to harm her reputation or take a chance of…."

"Where have you gone, Ben? You look so very far away."

"Nowhere love, I was just thinking about a conversation with my coach about you and me."

"Did he warn you about me, Ben?"

"Yes Angel, but I assured him we were careful, and our relationship was completely platonic. Though God knows it gets harder each day to keep it that way."

"Ben my father says in the Native culture I became a woman on my fifteenth birthday, but I know what the laws are here in Illinois. I want you to know it is killing me too. Sometimes I feel as if time will be too short for us and we will regret some of the lost opportunity."

"Shush, nothing is ever lost. This year has given us a chance that most couples seldom have. The chance to get to know each other deeply. I don't regret them. Do you?"

"Absolutely not!"

Chapter Five

Her black braid flowed down her back as she raced bareback across the field. Ben found joy in the movement of the horse between his thighs as he watched Rebecca flying in front of him their bliss was indescribable. It was her eighteenth birthday and perhaps....

The wind whipped through her braid, pulling tendrils loose to wrap themselves around her face. Her laughter was contagious and yielded a glorious sound of joy. It must have been her Native American father who had taught her to ride. Rebecca laughed loudly. She could imagine Ben's thoughts as he trailed behind her.

God, he loved her. *I can't imagine a life without her in it.*

"I'll catch you yet!" he yelled, tapping his horse's flanks a little harder. The race was on; he knew Rebecca would win. For all his athletic prowess, Rebecca with her Native American blood and horse whisperer qualities was untouchable. *At least we'll meet at the lake;* Ben must have thought. His imagination must have been going wild with the thought of private time with his soon to be a bride. *I would never have believed she would choose me. After all, I am so much older than she is, and with her beauty and brains, she could have picked anyone younger and more handsome. Even Jamie has a crush on Rebecca, as young as he is. But I'm the one she selected.*

When he finally caught up to her as they neared the lake, she was laughing that joyful tinkling sound that ripped through Ben's heart. *God, I can barely think when she looks at me like that,* he thought. His heart was pounding, and the heat was rising in his body as he jumped from his horse and pulled her into his arms. The hotness of the summer sun, mingled with the smell of horses, sweat, and woman filled his senses. "Rebecca, I swear you put a spell on me."

She threw her head back and laughed. The last of her hair slipped out of the braids, cascading down her back. "Ben, if I were to put a spell on you, I promise you'd never even suspect it. Although, we don't put spells on people. It is not in our beliefs," she said earnestly.

"Oh, I know you don't, my love, but it truly feels like I was mesmerized the moment I laid eyes on you," Ben tenderly said, as he pulled her to the ground, his arms cradling her.

Their horses had wandered over to the lake and were drinking the fresh, clear water as the two lovers sat, watching. Neither of them needed words. The moment was rich in its beauty and quiet peacefulness. An occasional seagull flew across the lake, and birds chirped loudly in the trees, flitting among the branches.

"It's all perfect, Ben," Rebecca said quietly. Her voice was but a whisper, not wanting to disturb the beauty of nature around them. Her pearl engagement ring shone creamy against her burnished finger.

"When can we announce it, Rebecca? I want to shout it to the world—not hide it in the shadows. I believe even Jamie will be happy for us, or as happy as he can be when he wishes it would be him, instead of me. And my folks will be excited. They love you as a daughter already. Becca are you sure about us?"

She took his hand, rubbed her thumb along the lines of his big palm. "Surer than I've ever been about anything, Ben.

I know my father had wished me to marry into the tribe. He is, after all, a shaman, and though not a cynic nor bigoted, he sometimes sees the future possibilities. He believes a daughter of my body will contain the magic of the old ones. He'd like to have that promise be a part of the tribe. I don't believe it has anything to do with you, Ben. But I know even though he might wish I was marrying into her father's tribe, he is a realist and knows that will not happen."

"I don't understand his point of view, Rebecca. After all, he married outside the tribe. Ana is an Irish Celt; she isn't Native American."

"I think that is a part of the magic I am supposed to pass down, Ben. The magic of three peoples. My father knows this even though he would prefer it to be different."

"My ancestors came from Africa, and we have our share of magical ceremonies too. Of course, I'm so many generations removed that I don't have a clue what they are."

"But, Ben, the magic is still in you, as it is in me, my father, and my mother. My father understands this."

Ben reached over and cupped her face in his big hands. Their eyes met and smiled, as his lips moved toward hers. The sound of a horse's hooves shuffled behind them.

Chapter Six

"Ben, Rebecca, come quickly!" Jamie yelled. "Something's happened to your father, Rebecca."

"Jamie, what's happened?" Rebecca screamed as she pulled herself up onto her horse. "How did you find us?"

"There is no time for that. I'll tell you later. We must go and quickly." He turned his mount and headed back to town.

Dripping with sweat, the three of them dismounted at the stables. "Tell me what's happened, Jamie, please!" she begged.

"In a minute, Rebecca. My car is over there. I'll tell you on the way to the hospital." *Only someone with Jamie's fathers standing could have managed to get him a license to drive at thirteen. Yet it is lucky for everyone that he had one.* Ben thought.

"The hospital!" shrieked Rebecca.

Ben took her hand, and they ran after Jamie. As they piled into his shiny, red Jaguar XJR and slammed the doors, Jamie began talking immediately.

"Rebecca, there is a cooler in the back seat with some water and towels. Your father had a heart attack. He is in surgery now. Ana is beside herself with worry. She couldn't reach either of you, so she called me." He pushed his foot down on the accelerator.

"Faster, Jamie," she pleaded.

"I'm sorry. I don't dare go faster. If I get stopped, it will cost us even more time."

Ben reached for her, and she fell into his massive brown arms. "Please, let him be okay," she prayed.

Ben and Jamie looked at each other across her head. The look on Jamie's face told Ben a story he didn't want to hear, but knew would come. All that they heard above the sound of the tires on the pavement and the hum of the powerful engine was Rebecca's weeping. The trees gave the impression of whipping by them, as the car sped down the road. Still, neither man knew how to help her. Both of them understood that she knew that the worst was yet to come. The loss of her father would be heartbreaking to Ana, Rebecca, and the entire tribe.

With a slight skid, Jamie pulled in front of the emergency room of Northwestern Memorial Hospital. "I'll park and meet you inside," was all he said as they jumped from the car and ran into the hospital.

Both looked like two savages who had come in from a war. Dirt streaked their faces from their horseback ride, sweat, and tears. Rebecca was near a breakdown when Ben stopped her. "Ana and your father will need us to be strong for them."

"Of course," she said, taking a deep breath to calm herself. 'Thank you, Ben."

Ana ran toward them and hurled herself into Rebecca's arms. The two women cried silently as their bodies shook with pent-up emotions.

For a few minutes, no one moved. Ben watched, and the women held each other until Ana looked up, saw Ben, and held out an arm for him. She recognized the loss he, too, would feel and pulled them all into the waiting room. Just then, Jamie walked back into the hospital. Ana and Rebecca held hands, as the four of them sat in the uncomfortable, green plastic chairs.

"We were having our afternoon cocktails, Rebecca,' Ana explained, 'and Kinard grabbed his chest, yelled, and fell over. From the moment we laid eyes on each other thirty years ago, he has always been my strength. I don't know what I can do. If he doesn't make it, how will I go on?"

"Mother, I don't know," Rebecca said simply, her hand giving Ana's a gentle squeeze. I wish I could light the sage sticks and call upon the gods to help Father, but it isn't possible here. All we can do is wait and pray."

"I know, dear one. Your father wanted to be a part of your baby's life and to perform your marriage ceremony. There was little else he talked of except to help you and Ben through the coming days."

"Please, momma, don't talk as if he were already gone."

"I'm sorry, Rebecca. But I tell you I feel his spirit here with us. The news will come soon now."

Rebecca sobbed and held her mother tighter. "NO! Please, NO!"

"Hush, dear,' Ana said. 'Your father will only be gone in body—not spirit. He will not leave us."

Ben and Jamie sat silently watching the two women. They knew that there was little they could do at that moment. Soon they would be needed, but for now, just their presence was all they had to offer.

Chapter Seven

"Can't you see it, Ben? These tenthers are trying to take down the country's Constitution. Have you heard of Judge Janice Rogers Brown? She may be the proudest, most arrogant, insensitive tenther in the judiciary system. My God, Ben, she once compared being a liberal to slavery and Social Security to a socialist revolution. Now that she's made it into the elite society, she no longer cares what happened to her ancestors in Alabama. Some of the Tea Partiers, those running for the presidency, would elevate her to the federal bench. I am sure, and then nominate her to the Supreme Court if one of them gets elected. There is a real movement going on in some of these extremists' right wing 'conservative' groups."

"This Tea Party they formed sounds exactly like The American Liberty League and the John Birch Society. Its values harken back to the Confederate rebellion. They even have a flag of their own in place of the United States flag. At least what they espouse is just like the fanaticism of the past. I'm telling you, it is scary, and I would put money on it that the Koch Brothers, the Mercer's, and possibly even the DuPont's have money backing it."

"Rebecca, these people won't get away with what you are saying." Ben countered naively. He still believed that if he continued to keep a positive attitude, it would make the bad in the world all go away.

"Ben, you need to read some of the things that are going on. There is a movement among some Americans to do away with all social programs, including Social Security, Medicare, Medicaid, Healthcare, OSHA, the child labor laws, and even the civil rights act. They want more and more guns on the streets, and it is beginning to appear there is an attempt to pit one race against another. It's a rational strategy when you consider that the basis for all their fear and anger about society is the fact that white males are no longer the majority of the population. The strategy is to divide and conquer. Make one nonwhite ethnic group angry at another. Make them forget they have strength in unity to change society for the better. Get them fighting among themselves, so they won't even notice the white male minority regains total control. I fear that the idiot real estate developer is going to run. Not that he is anything but a conman and unless I'm completely off base, there is some foreign power involved."

"Jamie," Ben said, turning to his friend. "What do you think? Do you think there is a chance of this all happening?"

"Well, Ben, I think Rebecca may be onto something. Some odd things are going on in this country and the world. Why I even hear some strange remarks from my father now and then."

"Like what, Jamie?"

"Ron Paul recently argued, 'The beneficial, educational impact of the John Birch Society over the past four decades would be hard to overestimate.

It is certainly far more than most people realize. Anyone who has been in the trenches over the years battling on any of the major issues—whether it's pro-life, gun rights, property rights, taxes, government spending, regulation, national security, privacy, national sovereignty, the United Nations, foreign aid—knows that members of the John Birch Society are always in there doing the heavy lifting. And most importantly, they all appear to approach these issues from a strong moral and constitutional perspective. At least that is how they talk. But I've read the constitution, and I do not see what they are doing as constitutional."

Rebecca interrupted, "Lots of people pay lip service to the Constitution, but Birchers study it, understand it and twist it into something they can apply to turn our society into a model of the Russian oligarchy. They aren't serious about protecting the Constitution and holding public officials accountable to it. And we all know what the John Birch Society stood for in the sixties and still does today. It is all that 'give to the rich at the expense of the poor' crap. Oh, and trickle-down economics as if THAT ever worked. It's just another pretend game geared for the sound bite."

"I don't know, sweetheart, if it is as serious as all that."

"Don't you get all condescending with me, Ben. It is, after all, my field we are talking about. And what about the white militia groups armed to the teeth ready to fight against our government? Remember Timothy McVeigh? He got caught, but the rest of his team is still out there somewhere—at least that's what his lawyer said after his client was executed, and he was no longer bound by attorney-client privilege.

Then the group out in Burns, Oregon, claiming to be honest ranchers fighting for ranchers' rights—did you see any diversity in that group? It's because it was a white militia group armed and trying to overturn Federal law while holding a copy of the Constitution in front of the television cameras. Are you surprised white supremacists and neo-Nazis fund these white militia groups?"

"I know you are both right, but I still don't get the why Rebecca," Ben stated, shaking his head.

"Ben, don't you understand, they don't care about the elderly, poor or the children. All they want is to own them, for their labor force and wars. They'd rather have them illiterate that's why they want to disband the department of public education and make it impossible for anyone without money to get an education. It's easier to control those who have never learned to think."

"Do you think it has come to this already Rebecca?"

"It is getting there Ben. When you disavow science, math and make sure that the only ones that can read are those few who decide what can be learned, you squash the ability to question and think.

Many are calling for the children to learn through an apprenticeship, they reason that these children need only to learn a trade, and don't need to learn to read, write, science, or math."

"Isn't that almost child labor Rebecca?" Ben asked.

"Exactly Ben and free labor too, it only costs a few rags for their backs and a bit of food."

"What will happen to them when these children grow up? Ben asked seriously.

"I think they will wear a uniform and go to war Ben, and this horror of a man, who is running for President, is stirring up more and more anger, in 'an us against them sort of way.' Can you believe it? A reality star, with multiple bankruptcies, and not one iota of common decency might just make it to the White House." God forbid, if that happens we are all in for a very long dark time."

"Hey, you two! Enough politics for one day, please. Let's go do something fun. My brain is spinning already. Or at least let's talk about something else for a while." Jamie piped in, a worried expression on his young face.

"Okay, I agree. Why don't you boys go and do some man things for a while? I have a bit of studying to do anyway. I may even pick the judge's brain a little too."

"Ha, Rebecca, my dad would love that. He adores you."

"Do you think he would listen, Ben?"

"I am sure of it, honey. He is always talking about these things. Are you coming for dinner tonight?"

"I'll be there, my love heart. I can hardly wait."

"Then I'll see you later honey." Ben hugged his fiancée before the two young men walked out of the diner.

Chapter Eight

"Can you just imagine that conversation, back in the 1930's, Judge, when they were all planning that coup?"

"I have read about it and see many similarities between what is happening today and what happened then, but I must admit I never thought about actual conversations," Ben's father said quietly in response.

"Stuart, do we need to discuss this at the dinner table?" Lisa asked quietly, her lovely brown face covered in concern.

"She's been talking about nothing else for days," Ben said.

"Well then, why don't we hear her out a bit," Stuart said, glancing around at his family. *The blue and gold china look nice on the table, and, as usual, Lisa has outdone herself with the dinner,* he thought. *She will be unhappy with the turn of the conversation I'm sure. Still, with the way things are going, it must be talked about, and Rebecca has a good head on her and sees the bigger picture, more than most do.*

Chapter Nine

"Go ahead, Rebecca,' the judge said, 'let's hear what you think went on in that room in the 1930's. Please, tell us."

"Thank you, sir. I believe, it went something like this. They would all have been sitting in some gilded room someplace such as the Drake Hotel," Rebecca stated before she began weaving her story.

"Morgan might have said, 'Roosevelt must go. That is a given. He's simply unbelievable. He must be mad, going against his own kind like he is. Do you think it's polio affecting his mind?"

Irenee answered him nearly screaming. His voice was shrill with emotion. "We have all seen what men like Roosevelt and the Moran brothers stand for. It is absolutely beyond me; after all, we have nothing in common with this so-called common man, do we? The common man is less important than a foot soldier. After all, they have the intelligence of an ape, if they have that much. If they had any valuable traits whatsoever, they wouldn't be digging ditches and begging on the street. They are less important than the horses that plow the fields and, as such, are much less useful to us. They breed like rabbits and are fodder for us all. They ought to be in camps, after all, if one dies, there is always another to take his place."

'Pew said coldly, his low-pitched voice devoid of compassion, 'He's right, and we all know it. Keep them all poor and breeding. It gives us the cheap labor we need, and their children will take their place when they drop dead. Why should we care anyway? It's not as if they are human."

Chafee broke into the conversation, "Okay, gentlemen, we all agree our fortunes depend on this, and we know that this 'New Deal' of his will only ruin us and our business—not to mention what it will do to the fortunes we want to leave to our children. Jeffreys, do you think that we can trust this McGuire? Do you think we should talk to Howard Moran? He is, after all, a banker and is trusted by the masses, especially since he began giving them home loans."

"Not Moran,' came a voice out of the shadows. 'He is a fool! And that fool paid off those who invested with him out of his own fortune. Remember, his brother, Herman, is also the head of the Secret Service. No, Moran will not do at all. The family has that "noblesse obliges" thing going. Their stupidity is beyond me."

Morgan took another sip of his cognac. The Rouyer, Guillet & Cie Grande Champagne Cognac was the finest available in the present day's market, and Morgan liked his pleasures. Warming the thin blue balloon glass in his left hand, he picked up his Cuban Peacemaker cigar and took a long drag. "Ah yes, 'noblesse obliges.' None of it makes any sense to me either.

On the other hand, McGuire will do nicely. He isn't one of us, though he wants to be. He has a family to feed, and even though he's one of the dirty Irish—or maybe I should say because he's one of the dirty Irish—he can be bought. After all, he is just another foot soldier, and like all of the populous, he'll do whatever it takes for the money."

Cigar smoke filled the dim room in the Drake Hotel as the ten men sat, smoked, drank, and planned their coup. Dressed in a black suit and white gloves, a small black man served more cognac. Another taller, dark-skinned man carried a box of Cuban cigars around the room.

Charles Chafee coughed as he breathed in the heavy smoke in the closed room. The smoke, along with the thick, red drapes gave the chamber a claustrophobic feeling, even though the room itself was enormous. Its opulence was something that was only available in the best of the suites. The penthouse suite did not have copies of masters' artworks on the walls. They were the real things. The tables were hand carved, and the walls covered in the finest of gilded paper. "Should we bring McGuire in then? Are we ready, or is there more we need to discuss first?" Charles asked the other men sitting around the room in their overstuffed chairs.

"Not yet, Charles,' Davis answered and then turned to the group and asked, 'which organizations do we have control of for our propaganda machine at this point? Who has the list?"

"You're right,' Charles responded. 'Let's make sure we have all the other pieces in place before we bring in our new minion. We have the American Liberty League, The Southern Committee to Uphold the Constitution—Irenee, we all know your family is the main financier of that one. There are also the Sentinels of the Republic, and the Crusaders, which J. H. and Vance control. Then, of course, the Black Legion.' He chuckled. 'Well, it is aptly named as its run by members of the Klu Klux Klan and prevents unionizing. I do so like to hear those stories," Charles finished.

"But to make it all work,' Davis added, 'we need the Veterans on our side for Roosevelt's actual overthrow, we must promise them their bonuses, help with their education and healthcare. Of course, it will be lip service. You're all wondering why we should waste the money on them. If they were worth anything but fighting, they would have bought their way out. But we need to make the promises anyway to get them on our side."

Chapter Ten

"Well,' Jeffreys said as he turned to the shorter of the two servants and nodded, 'let's bring him in then. I believe we all agree he is our man.'

McGuire walked into the smoke-filled room. He caught his breath and tried not to gasp or cough as the cigar smoke nearly choked him. The smoke combined with the heavy smell of cognac permeating all around him. He fought to conquer the dizziness in his head and struggled to hold back the queasiness in his stomach. It had been a long time since he had visited a speakeasy. He'd had some fun days in them in the past, but now he had a wife and children to consider. He much preferred to spend each moment that he could spare with his family. Money had been tight for him and his family since the stock market fell in 1929 and made it difficult to find money to save for anything other than the necessities of life. He considered it a blessing that he'd had the foresight to take care of the clothing he had bought earlier in his life. He had bought well and now looked presentable at this meeting. He clasped his hands behind his back to control their trembling as he walked further into the room. *Lord, what a collection of men,* he thought. *You could pay the salaries of every man, woman and child in the entire country with the money these ten men had.*

"Get in here, McGuire,' Morgan ordered. 'What are you dawdling for? Gentlemen, McGuire will work out fine for our purposes. He was a bond salesman, and as such it will be easy for him to explain large sums of money going in and out of his hands."

"You won't find it difficult to travel, will you, McGuire?" Chafee asked.

"No, sir, I won't. And I promised my wife a trip abroad before the crash, so she will be happy and won't question anything."

"Chafee nodded in agreement. 'Good then. I know Morgan already explained some of what we expect of you.'

"Yes, sir, I do. Although, I'm a bit unclear on why we need a military man involved."

"A high-pitched voice from across the room interrupted the conversation. 'Charles, I'll explain to him what he needs to know for now.'

McGuire turned his eyes to the big, well-dressed man across the smoky room. *His clothes may be worth a fortune,* he thought, *but they hang on him like rags. Some people, no matter how expensive their clothing, look sloppy and crude.* As his eyes narrowed a bit trying to see through the smoke, McGuire realized the man was Mr. Jeffreys. *Oh my god! He could buy and sell everyone in this room if he wanted.*

Jeffreys continued, 'McGuire, in order to save the United States of America from Franklin Roosevelt and his New Deal, we must have the military behind us. We can't get the active duty military at this time, but we can get the veterans. They are quite disillusioned with Congress' lack of voting on the promised bonus."

"Yes, yes, it is true,' Irenee added. 'With the right General officer helping, we will be able to get the veterans behind us."

Morgan interrupted, "We all have supported their groups for a while now. Of course, they don't know that. Nor do they realize we have also paid some members of Congress to vote against their bonus."

McGuire's eyes flitted from one man to another as each spoke in turn. Some of these men he didn't know, and, of course, he hadn't been introduced. He thought, *I expect they consider it unimportant for me to know them.*

"Pull up a chair, McGuire,' Charles said huffily. We can't have a real meeting with you standing.' A snap of his fingers brought one of the servants over, carrying a straight-backed chair.

Sitting down, McGuire thought, *one can tell I am not a part of this group just by my chair.*

Charles went on without a thought for McGuire's comfort. 'Who do you like, McGuire?

You are closer to the common man than any of us are."

"Sir, I truly believe the right man for this job is General Smedley Butler."

Morgan jumped in, "Isn't he a bit of a loose cannon?"

Jeffreys answered, "He tends to spout off without thinking of the consequences, and in public too."

"Yes, he does all that,' McGuire answered. 'Yet the men all love him. The lower ranking officers and even the non-commissioned soldiers trust him. They will follow him because they believe he has their best interests at heart."

Irenee yelled back, "He bothers me! I don't trust him. Do you believe he will go against the current status quo? Think, man! He supports Roosevelt!"

McGuire tried to keep his voice soft and calm as he explained himself. "If you listen to his speeches, he has become quite anti-establishment, and I happen to know that since he has retired, his pocketbook is suffering. Not that a soldier's pay, even a General's, is all that much to start with."

"Can we convince him to help us return to the gold standard?' Chaffee asked. 'Not to mention the overthrow itself? We'd best not bring up the overthrow until he is firmly in our pocket. And he damn well better keep his mouth shut about it."

"With the proper words, I believe we can convince him,' McGuire answered. 'I doubt he'd say anything about an overthrow since that would destroy him. What are the policies we intend to expose?"

Chapter Eleven

"You have spent a lot of time in Europe of late McGuire, what would you do?" Jeffrey's asked.

"If I were running a coup I would be taking the playbook from the Croix de feus. They have eight central policies in place. Which are:

1.) Restrict freedom of speech and stop the assembly of all those we dislike.

2.) Dissolve all labor unions.

3.) Privatize state monopolies and repealing social insurance laws.

4.) Stop all state "interference" in education. All technical schools would be run by big corporations.

5.) We must oppose state-planned economy

6.) Remove the trust of other countries,

7.) Mandatory 2-year military service and, of course, military spending must not be reduced.

8.) The public must make sacrifices as it did in France to end the financial problems, yes, they will scream a bit, but if we use the right propaganda, they will believe it is for their own good. After all, people will sacrifice a lot if they think someone else is sacrificing more.

The goal, of course, is to return our country to an aristocratic society that is the right and natural state of being." McGuire finished.

"You have it to a 'T' McGuire." Now back to the matter at hand. Can we count on General Smedley Butler?" Rockefeller asked.

"I do believe we can handle him; he is, after all, a man of the people. He needs to be shown the way and learn the importance of our views. I don't believe we should tell him the entire project at once though. It might not settle well with him if we do not do it in stages. He is, after all, an odd cat. It will, of course, help us that we have some of the newspapers on our side, it would be better if we controlled all of the media, but we don't presently.

The Quanah Tribune out in Texas, owned and operated by our friend Mr. Koch, is especially helpful." McGuire finished.

"It is settled then, off with you Jerry and let us know what you need to make it happen," du Pont stated, as he dismissed McGuire.

Silence filled the room, as each man sat sipping his brandy, thinking and waiting for McGuire to be out of earshot.

"We must get rid of Roosevelt, and we must get back on the right track. These dirty Irish immigrants and their ilk must not be allowed to bring down our country. What purpose do they have anyway, they are as much use to the world as the blacks and Indians are, only fit for menial labor.

This whole idea of giving the poor an education, teaching them, feeding them, helping their children and their old is so much bullshit." du Pont said icily. God help me, where on earth is this country going anyway. I thought we had the upper hand when we crashed the market and brought those ragamuffins down. Now Roosevelt and his bunch want to raise them up again. If we don't stop it soon, we will have everyone unionizing, going to school, and we will lose our workforce altogether."

"You have that right, of course, Irenee,' Pew stated coolly. 'While we are courting Butler, we should send McGuire to Germany and Italy; he can do a study of their use of the retired military in government and get a better understanding of what we must do."

"J.H. the unwashed poor will be the death of me yet, put them in labor camps, I say! If they cannot behave we exterminate them, what use do we have for discontents anyway? They are just vermin; you should come into my factories and see how well they run with my troops keeping the workers plugging away." Irenee stated.

"What do you think?" Rebecca asked nervously.

"I must admit it sounds very plausible Rebecca and I see so many of the so-called ideas that are being spouted today repeated in your vision of that conversation. Especially, the part where there is actual testimony concerning some of the things they stood for." Stuart said quietly, with an edge of anger in his voice.

"Do you think so, Dad? Ben asked, the Judge. 'I mean how can it be happening today?"

"Ben, I believe it would be easier today than in the nineteen thirties', what with so much of the media owned by corporations that are run by many of the children and grandchildren of those who planned the coupe in nineteen thirty. Not to mention what went on with the John Birch Society in the sixties, the Koch's were a big part of that, and much of the language is the same. Do you have an imaginary scene for that boardroom Rebecca?" The Judge asked earnestly.

"I do sir but am hesitant."

Chapter Twelve

"Oh, my dear girl, please understand, I am not making fun, it is an honest question. Putting the pieces together sometimes requires someone with imagination who can see the big picture."

"Well then here is what I believe happened or something similar." She said as she began to weave another story.

"We have been working on another way since Butler brought down the coup in nineteen hundred and thirty-three." Stated Henry Koch to the group of men sitting in the brightly lit boardroom.

"That's all well and good to say, but what exactly have we been successful at lately?" Barry said interrupting. "After all it didn't help me get elected did it? Now we are stuck with LBJ; possibly we can run Wallace one day."

"Patience Barry," Welch said. "You might not have gotten in, and that is unfortunate. However, we do understand now that we need to begin to put our people in more areas of government. To get our agenda done, will take more time than we expected."

"I do hope we don't have long to wait." Major General Walker stated.

"I believe we can do it in our lifetime gentlemen, but if not at least in our children's." Koch went on. "We need more control of the media, put education back into the private sector, above all get rid of public education, teach them a trade and war. That is all the 'common man' is good for. We must have our people in all of the government offices and of course the judiciary system too. I believe we can even con Hollywood into helping our cause if done correctly. After all, the propaganda worked for Hitler, it may take longer in this country, because of the stupid system we currently have in place. We will have to pit one group against the other, start small with local elections and move those who believe in our goals up into the hierarchy."

"He is right Barry, our biggest problem is the unions, women, and education. Undocumented workers will help bring down costs for us until we can ship the jobs overseas. First, we must set up the system, so we don't pay an arm and a leg in import taxes. Then when jobs become scarce again, it will be the unions that will fall." Welch said firmly.

"Then what?" Barry asked.

"Along with all of that, we must take over the justice system and spark the religious zealots to fight. It will come. Time is on our side." Walker finished.

"Becca I can see the correlation between what you are saying and what is happening today. I get so angry when I see, over and over some appellate court judge appointed by this bigoted, narcissistic man, who is in the White House, overturns another of my decisions in favor of a corporation. Not to mention we do appear to be going backward with civil rights too."

"And women's rights, environmental rights, and everything else that keeps us healthy too. Then there is that whole kneeling thing, making the National

Anthem into a way to stop first amendment rights too. You know what I mean about that Ben!"

"Becca, I tried to stay neutral on the anthem thing, but it's no longer possible. When the President is making it about suppressing freedom of speech and peaceful protest, all to incite his base, those who hate anyone that doesn't look, believe, dress or act as they do, even I can't be silent."

"You see it now Ben?"

"Yes honey, as much as I try to keep my head in the sand, there are some things even I can see that aren't right."

Chapter Thirteen

"Oh, Ben, isn't she beautiful?"

"She has your green eyes and glorious cheekbones, darling," Ben said, kissing Rebecca.

"I think she has your mouth, Ben,' she said, smiling as the baby gurgled and played with her toes. 'I wish your parents were alive to see her."

How perfect they are, Ana thought, looking in at her small family. *I wish they'd all have more time. But, we must take the happiness now while we can.* She walked into the room with a bright smile on her face.

"Can I join you, my darlings?"

"Of course, momma. Ben and I wouldn't have it any other way."

"Soon she'll be walking and talking up a storm. Jewell is the perfect name for her,' Ana said, admiring her little granddaughter. 'I wish all her grandparents were here to teach her some of their wisdom."

"So, do we momma," Rebecca said sadly, looking around their beautiful home, and seeing the sorrow tinging her mother's smiling face, as she played with Jewell. *The country was almost unrecognizable now; he had succeeded in inciting enough riots to declare martial law. After that, with the help of Russia and their bot farms, things went from bad to worse. The downtown area of Chicago was walled off. The poor, and people of color, were forced from their homes into the gutter buildings. The Army put them up after tearing down the rest of the city. Soon, I know he will disband Congress.* she thought.

"There is bottles and baby food in the fridge my darlings. Jewell is past breastfeeding now, and I have to go." Rebecca said quietly.

"Not into the lower town again Rebecca?" Ben pleaded. The last two times they warned you. I fear, what will happen if you go again."

"Darling Ben, it is my destiny. I must keep up the fight. It is important, to teach the women, children and the poor. There is no hope for our future if I don't. When the time comes that they take me away Ben, you must denounce me and take Jewell into the lower town and hide."

"Rebecca, I can't, I just can't."

"You must Ben; it will be all that will keep Jewell safe. It will be the only hope for our country."

Openly crying now, Ben could not form the words that would save her.

"It's not just that Ben, they would come for us even if I didn't do anything. We are not their kind. We are not white, nor do we follow their brand of Christianity. Please, darling," she said, as she stroked his face with both hands and kissed him gently.

"Ben you know I am right. With the current state of our country, and you unable to even play football anymore, just because you are not white. I have to do what I can, we all do."

'They will take me this time if they catch me. I am sure of that. It will be the worst days of my life, but without it happening, our country is doomed.

When I am gone, you must take Jewell first to the place Catherine set up and after that Jamie has promised to relocate you and Jewell to the lower towns. Everyone must forget that we were ever connected. It is the only way, my love."

"Ben, Kinnaird and I saw this many years ago. I don't want it to happen any more than you do. But it is her destiny, just as it is Jewell's to grow up to be the catalyst to remake our world." Ana stated, with tears running down her cheeks.

"Why can't we all disappear out to the country as some have. I hear there are those living off the grid, farming and living in the open. Yes, I know the water is not what it once was, and even the dirty air from the cities finds its way out there sometimes. But, it wouldn't be slavery."

"I wish we could go, my love, but it is the white folks, who don't stand out and the Native American's who remember their traditions and can melt into the landscape. It wouldn't be us, and it wouldn't help the world.' Rebecca said flatly, and even though she knew the pain would be unbearable for Ben, she finished her statement. 'It wouldn't help us any more than it helped your parents Ben. They killed them outright, and you know it."

Ben winced, as her words struck a blow to his heart.

'Mother, you must go now. You must do your part to make things ready, for the time when Jewell is fifteen. Ana and I have taught her all we can for now. Ben, you must continue it, and you will have a lot of help from unexpected sources. I know she is still a baby, but Catherine will help you for a time, my love. I wish I could be with her to teach her more, but what I have given her will have to suffice. The quiet and solitude that Jewell will have will lead her more swiftly than any of us know into the between times. She will master it and more."

Chapter Fourteen

The whip swung through the air and landed so hard on Rebecca's back, it dug deep into her tender flesh, and she awoke from her daydream.

"Well, it's about time I got your attention," Burrows sneered loudly.

Not a sound could be heard from the crowd. It was silent. A terrible, fiery agony spread across Rebecca's back, her flesh hung in ribbons, blood covering her back and running down her legs.

The last shreds of cloth, lying on a heap on the ground covered in blood. Rebecca swooned.

"Oh no you won't, hose her down. Burrows said. Today's games aren't over yet, especially since she didn't make one tiny sound."

Ten men ran out of the door, carrying hoses. After the first blast of water hit her, she woke up. But it didn't stop there; water poured over her, pounded on her back and mixed with her blood. It ran in funnels onto the ground. Though it soothed the dreadful torment, it brought her back from the past, and she was again in the courtyard.

"Put something on her back, so she stops bleeding all over the place and turn her around and keep her tied between the poles. It seems that the whip won't break her, so let's have some real fun," Burrows yelled at the guards.

A cooling salve was applied to her back, though it stopped some of the agony and most of the bleeding, it left her entirely at the mercy of whatever someone wanted to do to her. For the first time, Rebecca felt utterly vulnerable.

All the while, they were cleaning her up a bit, refreshments were served to those in the crowded gallery. She looked up and wished she hadn't. Many of the men had their pants open today in preparation. Their male organs were rising in the sunlight as a tribute to the games that were about to begin.

Some were sipping beer or wine and eating popcorn or hotdogs. But, nearly all of them had their pants open to the afternoon sun.

I can't stand it, not this, PLEASE not this. Rebecca's mind screamed.

Burrows walked over and slid his hand under her chin, caressing her bruised cheek. The other hand behind her head as he pulled her into him and stuck his tongue down her throat.

Stepping back, he slapped her as hard as he could. "If I kiss you, next time YOU will kiss me back."

"NEVER!!" Rebecca answered. Only to be hit this time with his fist, breaking her cheekbone.

She struggled to screams of mirth from the bleachers and sagged once again, passing out.

"HOSE her down!"

Again, she woke to the pounding of water, bringing her back to the now.

Burrows stood so close, to her that if she was loose, she could have kicked him and run, but she was tied spread-eagled, nude. Rebecca nearly gagged at the smell of his breath and for the first time noticed his rotten teeth, yellowed and black-toothed smile. It horrified her as he moved closer. His hands teased her nipples and slid in and out of her most private parts. Caressing every inch of her body, all the while making sure that the crowd could see every move that he made. He knew they were filming everything and it was live on the air for all to watch. At least all who had television nowadays. He would do this right, oh how he loved an audience.

Again, she swooned and awoke to the thunderous pounding of water. But this time, she was lying on a dirty mattress, someone had thrown on the ground, and being raped.

How many times and how many men raped her she didn't know, she blanked out again, sinking into her memories. Her body helpless to stop the torture, but she didn't let them steal her soul or her mind. She departed into the past.

Chapter Fifteen

Ben watched the soldiers drag his wife up onto the scaffolding. The tall, muscular man hunched his back, so he didn't tower over the crowd. Rebecca's long black hair hung over her bruised and bloodied face, her dress stained with gore and soiled with rat droppings.

"I don't think I can do it, Jamie." His voice was nearly a whimper.

The tall, slender, redhead standing next to him, his hair hidden under a cap, which shadowed his face, put a hand on his shoulder and said. "You promised her Ben; she needs you here for moral support."

"God, I know, and neither of us can be seen here either Jamie. Its Jewell's life at risk, should one of us be recognized. I promised Rebecca to protect Jewell. Oh God Jamie, look at her, they beat her and worse." His quiet voice racked with pain, tears streaming down his face, Ben slumped into his friend.

"Here ye,' Here ye," shouted the magistrate to the assembled crowd. "This woman was found guilty of disobeying the new laws. She left the upper town of her own accord and was caught teaching the women and children of the lower town. We all know women are not teachable, they are not as men. Women are the servants and slaves of men. Her punishment will be substantial, it will serve to teach you all, the law is not to be trifled with, and it will not be broken."

"Will you renounce your delusions, Rebecca and take the rightful place of a woman? Speak woman." Said Burrows.

The silence was deafening, except for the quiet sobs, there was nothing until Rebecca pulled herself up to her full height and spoke.

"In the dark days of the United States of America, a girl will be born. She will have the

power to make people fade from sight. Sound will disappear with a wave of her hand.

She will have the power to control the between times, and during that time, the girl child will call to her all the spirits of the past, present, and future. They will come and join hands with her. Together they will become one power, one body, and that body shall control the magic of the between times. From that day forward, the darkness and despair will disappear from our country. The world will be made new, and all people will once again be equal under the eyes of the law. Kindness will return to our society. Men and women will no longer be the property of the rich.

Corporations will no longer have the power to dictate the lives of their employees, forcing them to remain stuck in a life of drudgery. Money will be made in abundance, but not at the expense of the lives of others. The American dream will return."

"SHUT THE F… UP BITCH!" Screamed one of the guards as his fist brutally landed on her face.

Chapter Sixteen

Ben nearly swooned, burying his face in that of his friends. "Oh God, Oh God, I can't stand it!

"Where is Jewell, Jamie? Is she safe? She is so small; I couldn't bring her here, and even if she were older, I couldn't let her watch her mother burn,' the big man sobbed, his entire body a quivering mass of flesh. 'How am I to take care of her and keep her safe in this hell hole that has become the lower town?"

"Shush, Ben, she is with my sister Catherine. We couldn't let her go with Rebecca's mother?"

"Ana, she disappeared, right after they took Rebecca, is she still alive?'

"Yes,' Jamie whispered. 'Let's hope she can stay alive. I'll tell you about it later. My God, Ben, we have to leave now. They are watching us. Be quiet and put your head down. Don't say a word, keep walking. Trust me, Ben. Jewell will be back tonight. For now, I'm with you, Ben."

"Until Jewell is a bit older, you'll have you stay in the upper town. It will be difficult for me to talk them into letting you stay in the upper town, but I can manage it for a time, by convincing them that the people in the lower town must forget you. You must denounce Rebecca loudly."

"I can't do that Jamie."

"It is vital for Jewell and the prophecy that you do Ben. Don't forget you promised Rebecca."

"How can I forget that Jamie, she forced me to promise."

"As for me, I need to figure out a way in and out of the upper town," he said pulling the grieving man through the crowd. Ben put your head down man; they'll make us both."

The cold and darkness of the day crept into her soul, filling the empty spaces with the horror of what she was about to lose. Her body became ravaged by the fire as it licked up her legs, eating the bonds tying her hands. Her long black hair is alight with flames.

"Ben, remember!" Rebecca screamed. "The prophecy must be."

"NO!" He cried, as Jamie clamped his arms around his friend and held his face against his chest to stifle the screams.

Tighter, Jamie held Ben. The only thing that saved them was the swaying, moaning mob.

The poor souls, lost without hope, standing in the inundating, swelling mass of unwashed, hopeless humanity.

"Come on Ben. Jamie whispered. We have things to do, and you have a daughter to raise. The prophecy must come to pass. Heaven help us if it doesn't."

Still trembling the big man said, "I don't know if I can do it, Jamie."

"You will Ben, once you hold your daughter again, you will know what you need to do."

"Oh Jamie, how can a three-year-old take on all the chores she will need to?"

"She will learn with your help and the help of the between times Ben. She must, though I too am worried about that. The first thing is she will have to learn, is to be very quiet."

"God this is so awful Jamie, it is as if we are living in a nightmare. What has happened to the world?"

As they reached the outskirts of the horror and moaning mob, Ben once again clung to Jamie and sobbed Rebecca's name.

"Come with me Ben, for a few weeks after you denounce Rebecca, I will get you a job doing street cleaning. After that, you and Jewell will need to disappear into the lower town. Catherine will lead you through the tunnels, and then you must make your way to the apartment that will be your home. Rebecca left you directions to it didn't she?"

"Yes, but I haven't opened the letter yet."

"I cannot know where you live when you move into the lower village. But I will find a way to keep in contact."

Ben, you must grow your beard out and teach Jewell what she will need to survive when you are at work.

Remember never to mention who you once were to the people in the lower towns. They must forget who you were. We have to go now, Ben." Jamie said as they pulled their hoods further over their faces and disappeared into the fog.

Chapter Seventeen

As the weeks went on, Ben swept streets in the upper town. It had taken everything in him to denounce Rebecca to the authorities.

I can't believe the names I called her, he thought, as he walked to the tiny apartment that held Jewell and Catherine. These apartments were set aside for those working in the upper town. *Jewell and I would already be in the lower towns if it weren't for Jamie. The Upper Town was whites only.* They didn't want their workers to have contact with the lower towns. Not at this point Not while the unrest in the lower towns was still being sorted out.

"Hi ladies!" His voice whispered, as he entered the apartment. Jewell came flying into his arms, crying "Daddy" in her young voice.

"Shush, little one, you need to call him Father now.' Catherine spoke softly. 'Her cooking is coming along well. She can nearly sweep the floors by herself; I believe in another week she will be ready.

2

Ben, you can't stay in the upper town much longer. It's been nearly two years now, and things are getting worse for anyone who is not white."

"I can't carry the pails with water yet Father." Jewell said hanging her head low."

"That's alright daughter. Soon you will be able to do that too. Do you think she will be okay left alone for the ten or more hours that I am at work when we get to the lower town, Catherine?"

"We've been working on her weaving, and she has been learning to sit quietly in meditation. I believe she is as ready as can be Ben."

"I know we have to leave here soon, I've begun seeing the glances and whispers as I walk by, it isn't good," Ben stated softly.

"Ben, I think they are beginning to watch me too," Catherine said in a low voice. I fear soon they will follow me and then there will be no way for me to sneak you into the tunnels."

"How long do you think we have Catherine?" Ben asked shakily.

"No more than a few days to a week."

"Does it need to be tonight?"

"No! I believe we will have a few days to a week. During the days before I come to take you into the tunnels, Ben, I must not come here. Jewell will need to stay alone when you are at work."

"Jewell, do you think you are ready to get my dinner ready and stay noiselessly by yourself now?" Ben said quietly to his daughter.

Standing to her full height, his five-year-old daughter said, "Yes Father if I must." She said with a quiver of fear in her voice.

"You will have to be very silent Jewell."

"I know Father. She answered, shakily. I will have to be a grown-up now."

"Catherine, we will see you in a week or so then. Thank you for everything you have done for us and putting your own life on the line."

"I've only done what is right and necessary Ben, besides I love Jewell," she answered, as she swept the little girl into a hug. Holding on to Jewell, she whispered "You are strong enough young one, remember you are loved by many."

"I love you too Aunt Catherine," Jewell said in an uncommonly grown-up voice for such a small child.

As Catherine put Jewell down, she looked at Ben with tears in her eyes. "It's nearly curfew, and I must be home. When it's time, I'll come back, but it will be late at night. We will need the dark to cover ourselves from the sight of the police.

Sooner or later things will relax up here, but not for many years. Jamie has pulled a few strings through his contacts and gotten you a job in a factory in the lower town. Neither of us can know where you are living."

"Catherine, when do you think I'll see Jamie again?"

"Not for a while, he is still playing Papa's good soldier and setting up a disguise that will get him in and out of the upper town. It probably won't be for another year at the soonest, Ben."

"That long?"

"We can't take chances of leading anyone to you and Jewell. At some point, the whispers of Rebecca's prophecy will start some people wondering about Jewell. That is if it isn't happening already."

"I understand!" Ben whispered as Catherine shut the door gently behind her.

"Come, daughter, show me what you have made for supper."

As the two walked over to the small stove in the studio apartment, dread began to fill Ben.

I will pack up our things tonight so that we are ready, he thought.

Chapter Eighteen

Standing at the stove next to his daughter, Ben watched Jewell stir the oatmeal. She stood on a small stool, as she carefully stirred. Jewell made sure it didn't scorch the bottom or sides of the pan.

He would have to leave soon for his first day of work at the factory. It would be Jewell's first day alone in this small concrete basement room, with it's one small window. Her loom sat under the tiny basement window for the best light. In the center of the room, near the cook stove, stood a little table and two chairs. While Ben could barely put his legs under the table, Jewell had a large book she sat upon. He took in the beauty of his daughter, as he looked around the dark room.

At least it has the alcoves one for a privy and two sleeping areas, he thought. *There is still much to do to make it comfortable, but that will have to be done a little at a time.*

With care, the little girl carried a hot bowl of oatmeal over to him, before going back to get her smaller bowl. *As much as I want to, I know I can't help her. She must do this on her own,* he thought, longing to help his small child. "Daughter."

"Yes, Father?"

"I went out early and got the water for today. I believe I can sneak out a bit longer and do it, but you must work on getting stronger, I must not be caught going out in the between times."

"I will work on it everyday Father. Soon I will be able to do it and the washing too," she said bravely. 'I love you, Father; I will grow up quickly," she said, her arms around his neck.

Loosening her arms after squeezing them, Ben stood up. "I love you too daughter,' he said, as he made his way to the door. 'Now get out of sight until I lock the door behind me. I'll see you after work."

Jewell slid into the alcove and waited until she heard the lock click. Shivering in fear, she shrank into a small ball and sobbed. "I will be brave and strong. Jewell whispered quietly. I must be!"

PART II

Chapter One

"It's Father's early night at the factory, Sable," Jewell whispered to the small black cat circling her feet. Come, we must get into the shadows, Father will be home soon, and you know, how often he's told us we can't be seen. I do hope tonight; he will finally tell us why Mother had to die. After all, I am ten years old today and old enough to hear about it." "Sable, I don't want to listen to the gory details or listen to the horrible parts, but I must know the truth. I've felt Father's pain for so long, and I want to be able to help him through it. But I can't if I don't know what it's about.' The small girl finished. The dim light from the tiny coals in the stove brought out the red highlights in the long curly dark hair that framed her little face.

Sable slipped under the homespun black robe that covered Jewell's small body. "Father will be proud to hear that I was able to carry a full pail of water today. He won't have to take the chance of going out after curfew to replenish our water, Sable. Shush! Here he comes now. OH NO! It's not Father; it's that awful Youssef."

"Where is he? Youssef said, kicking the wall once again. I know it's that big black man's early shift. I need him to take my turn in the community garden tonight, he snarled. He'll do it or else...."

"Or else what?" Ben said, as his massive form materialized from the shadow at the side of the building.

"Well, you know Ben, I've been a bit sickly lately," whined the high-colored, black man. *If I'd just been born with my skin a smidgeon whiter, I might have lived in the upper town or at least in the white community. I hear they have it a little bit better than we do, he thought, Instead of this dump, we live in..*

"You are always sick Youssef, what do you want tonight? I've made plans tonight, and I have no time for your shenanigans."

"I bet it's with that pretty little girl of yours. What is she now about ten, nearly a woman isn't she?" he said with a sinister sneer.

"I'm warning you, leave her out of this. She's only a baby." Ben stated.

"Yeah, well I need your help tonight, and we both know what can happen if you don't do as I ask," Youssef said slyly.

"Do it yourself, Youssef or I'll do some reporting of my own" Ben stated, pushing past the skinny man. 'If you want my help, ask nicely next time and perhaps.... now get out of here, I want my dinner.'"

Muttering to himself, Youssef slunk around the corner.

Ben waited until the creep moved off. He knew Jewell would be hidden in the shadows, frightened by the exchange.

As the last slithering footsteps retreated, he opened the door to his basement flat, quickly entered and shut the door. His young daughter

2

threw herself in his arms before he was two steps inside the door. *Poor baby* he thought. *What a great birthday present she'd just been given with that conversation.*

Trembling, Jewell pulled away The small black cat still cuddled next to her bare feet. "It doesn't appear Sable has grown at all in the last three years, Jewel? But, look at you, almost a foot taller I'm sure."

"Father.' Jewell whispered, 'I have great news for you tonight and my first addition to our home too."

"Why it's me that gives you presents today, Daughter. It's your birthday, have you forgotten?"

"No father, I'm hoping tonight you'll tell me why mother had to die and why the world changed. I'm old enough now. Today I could carry a full bucket of water, and I've finished my first two tapestries. They're for the window and the door. But I need your help hanging them." She said in a hushed but excited voice.

"Goodness, you've been busy. I'm so proud of you Jewell. I know you've been working hard on carrying the water."

"Thank you, the pail is still heavy, but I don't spill even a drop now."

"I'm sure you don't sweetheart."

"Father, I wove the magic of the between times into the tapestries. They shut-out noise. No one will be able to hear us once you hang them up."

"Your mother, Grandmother, and Grandfather said you would be able to work with the between times. Do you know what the between times is Jewell?"

"I know it is the time of day when people's thoughts are quiet, and one can touch the good and the power in the universe Father. When I am one with the glory in the universe, I can pull into myself a part of that wonder and magic. It doesn't make me better than others, but it does make me stronger, and I am not alone. Instead, it seems that the silence and the universe fills me up and makes me more than myself. It runs through me, and into whatever I touch. Though, I expect I will learn more about it as I grow."

"Daughter that is already so much more than your mother knew or could explain to me. I have only a small ability to touch even a fraction of the between times. But then I am usually still asleep until dawn begins to break, even though it is still dark when I wake.

Now, why don't you show them to me, Jewell." Ben said as his daughter unfolded the small tapestries. A huge smile lit his face. White teeth gleamed in the light of the tiny coal fire, as his eyes glowed with the beauty his daughter had created.

"You like them, don't you father?" Jewell asked quietly.

"They are the most beautiful things I've ever seen Jewell.' His voice awed by the colors before him. 'I'll hang them now as you set dinner."

"Will you tell me about mother after dinner, Father?"

"I suspect it is time. His voice catching in his throat. 'However, did you manage to get the bit of thread I brought you to glow like this Jewell? Why, I know I never brought home emerald, green, gold, sapphire blue, and this majestic ruby red, not to mention the silver either. All I could find was the basic colors, drab blue, red, yellow, a bit of black and white." He said as he hung them. A tingle ran up his arms, as his fingers touched the cloth.

"It was the between times Father. I felt it run through me into my fingers and from them into the cloth. Somehow the colors just became what you see."

"The tapestries are glorious, dear heart,' he whispered quietly, a shine still in his eyes. 'If I buy you the thread can you make more? Jamie will buy them for a very high price I'm sure. They will give us a bit more coal for the winter, some warmer clothes too, nothing fancy, but a bit warmer and I can put a bit away for us to get away from here soon.

I hear that before things got bad, some folks escaped to the hills and are farming, with clean air and water or at least cleaner air and water than we have. I wish I could have taken you away, but your mother said we wouldn't make it, not being either white or Native American.

Oh, I know, it's a hard life, but they are free. They don't fear every day about where their food is coming from or if their sons will be taken away when they are six and daughters given away to whomever the magistrate chooses when they are fifteen. Jewell's face fell as he said the last words. I'm sorry sweetheart; I shouldn't have brought it up I know you are only ten today, but fifteenth must not seem that far away to you."

"It's okay Father, sometimes it feels as if it is a lifetime away, and at others, it seems as if it will be tomorrow, time passes so strangely. Except of course if I'm in the between times. The between times teaches me; it's how I know, I must learn quickly all you can tell me about my mother.

I need to understand, what happened to the world that I read about in the books you brought home. Why has the weather become so unbearable? The winters so frigid, the summers sweltering, and the storms so fierce. I'm sure even these people you talk about wouldn't have built the communities where they are if the lake had always risen high enough to flood the communities every time it storms.'"

Chapter Two

As the two of them ate the fried, left-over oatmeal from breakfast, the silence in the room was dreadful. The last of the coal still warmed the room, but a chill went through Ben as he ate. *I dread telling her how and why Rebecca died,* he thought.

Jewell, fearful of the horror she knew she would hear, anticipated the knowledge it would bring. *I must be strong and listen,* she thought.

"Why don't you sit nearer the fire Father, while I clean up the table," she said, pulling herself up to her full height.

The dank room darkened as the sun set, and the dimness made the tiny room smaller Ben pulled their chairs closer to the coal stove. *The bit of coal we are allowed doesn't take the dampness out of this place,* he thought, as he sat down and buried his head in his big hands and waited.

All too shortly, Jewell sat next to him; Sable curled on her lap ,as if she knew that comfort would be needed that night.

The silence dragged on. Finally, Ben coughed. "I guess, I should get started, Jewell.'

His daughter said nothing, but looked at him patiently, the expectation and fear in her small face made him wince.

"Before we talk about how Rebecca died," Ben said chocking on the words.

"Perhaps, I should ask you questions Father, and then you can answer them," Jewell said quietly, she knew there were probably other things she needed to know first anyway.

With a small sigh of relief, Ben said. "That would be best. You are wise little one."

"I think I need to understand why the world changed first. You told me that women used to vote and even hold public office. What happened and why are women not allowed to go to church, let alone go out in public, or meet each other? Why are we given away in marriage to someone, not of my choosing?

"Jewell that is a lot of questions, but I'll do my best to answer. Unfortunately, some men are afraid of women. They want to keep them as property and under control. Many of them consider women to be only for their pleasure and as a means of breeding their children."

"That is awful Father."

"Yes, it is and sad too."

"I guess those men got their way then?"

"Unfortunately, Jewell, they did. These men began to make laws to, as they put it, 'put women back in their place.' In the beginning, there was an effort to make the woman less important than the baby she might one day carry."

Looking up into the shadow of her father's face, Jewell said, "I read the biology books you gave me Father. Are you trying to say the cells that might become a baby are a baby?"

"I guess that is what they believed or at least that is what they used to confuse the less educated and others.' But science doesn't say that, so they began a propaganda campaign to make people think that science wasn't real and only religion knew the truth," Ben said, as he stood and put a tiny bit of coal into the stove. *It doesn't do much to light the room*, he thought, *but it keeps some of the chill out of the place.*

"That doesn't make sense Father, even in the Christian Bible talks about breath being life, and cells don't breathe."

"Correct."

"So, they must have started picking apart tiny little things in the Bible and redefining them to mean something they didn't mean." she said, her small hand petting Sable, a bit too quickly now.

"Yes."

"That is sad. But I don't understand why I am not allowed to pick my own husband or to go outside."

"As near as I can figure Jewell, these men figured that if women started talking to other women, they would begin to understand each other and revolt. Does that make sense?"

"I guess so. Do you mean that if women are locked up, don't see any of the world, kept uneducated baby machines and dying in childbirth, men can control them, and over time they too would believe they were not human?"

"Yes, I believe that is the case."

"How dreadful Father."

"But, it didn't stop there, they also had to target all religions that didn't agree with theirs and all people that didn't look like them," Ben said sadly. "Everyone had to be less than they were! That way they could control them. Keep them uneducated, except for what they wanted them to know. Keep each race separated from the others, to maintain the idea of 'them against us."

"Is that why the communities are divided up by race so that each type of community has only one race in it?"

"I believe so Jewell. I do hear that the poor white communities have things a bit better than the rest."

"Why Father?"

"It goes back many centuries Jewell, to the days when the white man came to this country, with the attitude that they were the master race. Some of the white race believes that if even the lowest white man knows that others have it worse, they are more complacent and will follow along."

"Seriously?"

"Unfortunately, yes that is how it appears to me and to those that knew much more than I do. Those who came before the turning.'

'Things were never the best for people of color in this country, Jewell, but we thought we were making progress. Women, blacks, Native Americans, and people of all races and religions could vote, go to school and make something of themselves. Or at least many of us thought they were improving."

"Father are you saying they weren't improving."

"Yes and no." What we didn't understand was the deep anger that boiled underneath the surface of many of the ill-educated white folks. Those that would rather see the end of the world, their family dead than have someone else doing better than they were. I guess in many ways, it goes back to the settlement of this country. To the time when natives and those brought from Africa in chains were considered by the elite white men to be less than human. After the Civil War, many in the south hated that they received the same wages as a black man and had to do the same work for those wages. That hatred never left this country; just buried deeper. If a person looked at it, they would see it in the Justice system's treatment of minorities, but not many talked about it."

'That answers many of my questions Father."

"But you have more?"

"Yes, Father."

"Go ahead, Daughter."

"I understand why those in power divided the different races into separate communities. And why they treat women the way they do. But, what has this to do with Mother?" Jewell asked.

"For you to understand, Jewell, you need to know what led up to everything."

He watched as she nodded before he went on.

"Father how sad it must be for people to need to have someone else be worse off than they are, to feel as if they are bigger people. It is backward in my thinking."

"In mine too,' he said, before going on. 'From what I have learned over the years, it took many generations for so many people to believe it was a reality."

"Father, how can what is reality be forgotten and what is fake become a reality?"

"Jewel, some politicians, and some religious leaders spread division among us. An 'us against them' propaganda, until too many became brainwashed into that mindset. Still, so many of us, me included, had to have it shoved in our faces before we believed our world would die as we knew it."

Jewell sat quietly listening; occasionally, her hand would pet Sable, needing the comfort.

"Go on please."

"The real beginning of the end for us was when a man ran for office and began calling all Mexicans drug dealers and murderers, mocking the disabled, calling the press FAKE if they didn't agree with him and otherwise sowing hatred everywhere. He said he was a plain-speaking man, who didn't believe in being politically correct. But the truth was, he was just a hate-filled man. One who is inferior to just about everyone I've ever known. But, he used the anger boiling underneath to incite people to hate more and follow him. This horrible man also had no regard for women and considered them to be his property to do with as he wished. He fed that belief to his followers along with the help of the elite in Russia and those countries who wanted democracy to die."

"But, why did so many people believe him?

"Dear heart, so many were apathetic and believed that all politicians were alike. They believed all the lies he told, and many held their noses and voted for him anyway."

"Why?

"Jewell, schools had stopped teaching enough about the importance of voting and how the different branches of the government worked."

"That is so sad Father. But that doesn't explain those who 'held their noses.'"

It came to light after the election that there was help from Russia and the all the cheating that had been going on for years, he took the Presidency. There was an investigation, and it was turning up a huge amount of corruption, but still, he had little to no opposition from his own party, which controlled both branches of our government."

"Father, if so much corruption was coming out from the investigation, why didn't anyone oppose him?"

"The Democrats did, and some of the Republican's talked a good game, but the Republicans by and large still voted for everything he wanted or refused to oppose him. Many of us thought that Russia had information on some in Congress too. But, I'm not sure about it." My God, Jewell, you are smarter at ten than I was at thirty."

"Is that when the poor lost the right to education?"

"Yes, and our air and water began to be further poisoned too."

"What else did he do?"

He began hiring the most unqualified, deplorable, lying people for his cabinet. Those that would help him dismantle all that was good in America. He waged trade wars and insulted our allies, and America began to die a little more each day. Food, jobs, and money became scarcer for most people, and the poorest of the poor perished or were jailed. Riots broke out on the streets, which finally brought about what he wanted."

"What did he want, Father?"

"Martial Law, Jewell. A way to finally separate the poor from the rich and get rid of anyone that disagreed with him for any reason. Your mother saw what was happening. When the army moved in, and began to create the upper and lower towns, the poor, women and children no longer had access to medical care, or schooling. Many of them died, and others relied on begging scraps from the rich. That is until the factories opened to produce trinkets and necessities for the rich and the war machine."

"Is that when Mother began going into the communities?" Jewell asked.

"Yes, Rebecca knew that it was imperative to teach and be a beacon of light to the poor"

"Do you think it helped the poor, Father? For my mother to sneak into the communities. "

"I don't know if it helped them, Jewell. I do know that she believed it to be her destiny and if she hadn't done it, there would have been no prophecy and no hope for any of us."

"What is the prophecy, Father?"

"The prophecy is that a young girl will be born who can use the magic of the between times and pull the spirits of all those of like minds from the past, present, and future to bring about change."

"Does that mean it is my destiny to fulfill the prophecy Father, I can pull in the between times and know that I will only get stronger as the years go by."

"I don't know for sure Jewell, but your mother, grandmother, and grandfather believed it would be you.' It is a dreadful burden for you to bear, sweetheart."

"Well, I'm not going to think about that part yet. I have much to learn, and perhaps there will be someone else when and if that time comes Father." Jewell said with wisdom beyond her years.

"It's probably best if you don't focus on the prophecy at this time Jewell."

"Father, why didn't anyone else fight this man?"

"As far as anyone fighting him, many, many did. That is why he had to get martial law. To get rid of those who resisted him and the investigations that were going on to find out and convict those who were guilty of conspiring with Russia. He also had to get rid of the Free Press and to stop anyone, including the resistance people, who didn't like him. It's been a long day." Ben said yawning.

She nodded as he stood, stretched, hugged her close and made his way to the privy and then to his bed.

Jewell sat quietly for a very long time, listening to her father snore, Sable purr, and thought about all she had heard. "Sable, I know I will think about my place in the prophecy Father told us about. But I must first put together all the pieces he has given me tonight. I must study, work in the between times, and read everything he brings home.

I know that Father is not ready to talk about how my Mother died, it may be years before he is. I'm alright with that for now. I know I have so much to learn first. Anyway, I'm not sure that it matters how she died. I understand why. I know what happened and I know what I must do. Does that make sense Sable?"

Sable's small black paw reached up and touched her face.

WHAT'S REAL AND NOT REAL

The attempted coup in 1933 to overthrow the government of the United States of America and President Franklin D. Roosevelt by a group of millionaires failed. The author used some of the congressional records, along with accounts from the book by Jules Archer, 'The Plot to Seize The White House: The Shocking True Story of the Conspiracy to Overthrow FDR,' to reconstruct fictional scenarios of what might have happened during this period. Some of the people involved can be found in documents in the Library of Congress, while others are purely fictional.

In the 1930s, the du Pont and Morgan family empires dominated the American corporate elite, and their representatives were central figures in organizing and funding the American Liberty League. The du Pont family was so complicit in this fascist organization that James Farley, FDR's postmaster general and one of his closest advisors, said the

American Liberty League "ought to be called the American Cellophane League" because "first it's a DuPont product and second, you can see right through it'" (Donald R. McCoy, Coming of Age). Gerard Colby, in his book DuPont Dynasty, outlines the family's pivotal role in creating and funding the League. The Dickstein-McCormack Committee learned that weapons and equipment for the fascist plotters' Croix de feu-like super army "could be obtained from the Remington Arms Co., on credit through the DuPonts." DuPont had acquired control of the arms company in 1932.

Irénée du Pont (1876-1963)
By Charles Higham

Irénée, the most imposing and influential member of the du Pont clan, was obsessed with Hitler's principles. He keenly followed the future Fuhrer's career in the 1920s. On Sept. 7, 1926, in a speech to the American Chemical Society, he advocated a race of supermen, to be achieved by injecting particular drugs into them in boyhood to make their characters to order. He insisted his men reach physical standards, equivalent to that of a Marine and have blood as pure as that in the veins of the Vikings. Even though he had Jewish blood in his running through his veins, his anti-Semitism matched that of Hitler.

In outright defiance of Roosevelt's desire to improve working conditions for the average man, GM and the Du Ponts instituted the speedup systems. These forced men to work at terrifying speeds on the assembly lines. Many died of the heat and pressure, increased by fear of losing their jobs. Irénée paid almost $1 million from his pocket for armed and gas-equipped stormtroopers, modeled on the Gestapo, to sweep through the plants and beat up anyone who proved rebellious. He hired the Pinkerton Agency to send its swarms of detectives through the whole [du Pont] chemicals, munitions and auto-empire to spy on left-wingers or other malcontents.

The formation of the American Liberty League, "to combat radicalism" and "defend and uphold the Constitution," was announced shortly afterward.

Heading and directing this organization were men from the du Pont and J.P. Morgan companies.

In 1934, several other pro-fascist organizations became active to combat the New Deal and the policies of FDR, but the most prominent was the recently formed America Liberty League. It was founded and supported by the Morgan's, the du Ponts, and the Pews, the Harriman's, the Mellon's, Remington, the Rockefellers, and other wealthy industrialists, per the 1947 investigation into Un-American Activities.

The American Liberty League propaganda said social security would "mark the end of democracy."

Although du Pont and J.P. Morgan companies were founders of the American Liberties League, no actual testimony that has been made public incriminating them or members of their family in the real conspiracy.

Harry Koch, the grandfather of Charles and David Koch, did own The Quanah Tribune in Texas.

The paper did do propaganda for the American Liberty League.

William (Herman) Moran was head of the Secret Service through five Presidencies, and the great, great-granduncle of the author.

Howard Moran was a prominent banker at the time, as well as Herman Moran's brother. He did pay off his clients with his fortune. He was the great, great grandfather of the author.

In 1958, the John Birch society was created. Its primary purpose was to limit government. Harry Lynde Bradley, the co-founder of the Allen Bradley Company and the Lynde and Harry Bradley Foundation, Fred C. Koch, founder of Koch Industries, Robert Waring Stoddard, President of Wyman-Gordon, a major industrial enterprise, were among the founding members. Another was Revilo P. Oliver, a University of Illinois professor. The society is still in existence today.

The Tenther movement is real, and its design is to bring more sovereignty back to the states and limit

Federal government involvement, including Fair Labor Laws, Child Labor Laws and Employee Safety Laws.

The Freedom Caucus, formerly called the Tea Baggers, and The Tea Party were all founded on the previous movements, and the Koch Brothers were one of the original backers of the movement. Just as the Koch brother's grandfather helped spread the propaganda of the America Liberty League, back in the 1930's, Charles and David Koch helped fund the Tea Bagger a.k.a. Tea Party a.k.a. Freedom Caucus movement.

A man was elected to office who is and has put into place a cabinet designed to do away with all regulations, including those for clean air and water. Education for the poor and middle class is under assault, as are Social Security and Medicare. Women's health, affordable health care for all but the wealthiest among us, voting rights, and the rights of the minorities.

The press and the rule of law are under attack today.

This book is a work of fiction, the names, places, and people are all fictional, except for those that are from public records.